Responding to BAD MANNERS

Learning to be POLITE

Jasmine Brooke

FOX EYE
PUBLISHING

Elephant sometimes forgot to be **POLITE**.

He could sometimes be a little **RUDE**.

He often forgot to say **PLEASE**. He didn't remember to say **THANK YOU**.

When Elephant was **RUDE** it sometimes **UPSET** others. That got Elephant into trouble.

When it was story time at school, Mrs Tree asked everyone to sit nicely on their chairs. She asked them to listen carefully. That was the **POLITE** thing to do.

But Elephant wriggled on his chair and he whistled a tune. That was not **POLITE**. It was a **RUDE** thing to do.

At lunchtime, everyone queued up to choose their food. Giraffe waited patiently. Gorilla said, "Yes, **PLEASE**." Monkey said, "**THANK YOU**."

But Elephant didn't wait.
He charged to the front
of the queue. He didn't ask
nicely and he didn't say
THANK YOU. It was not
the **POLITE** thing to do.

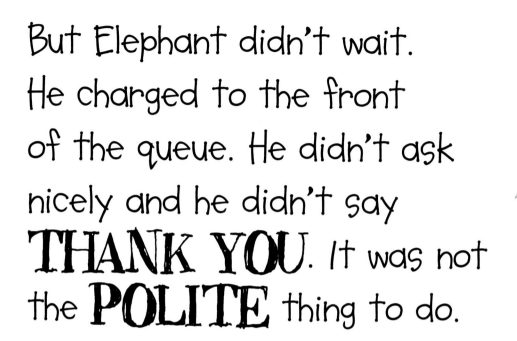

During the art lesson, Mrs Tree said everyone could paint. Elephant grabbed the red and the yellow. He took the green and the blue. He didn't ask nicely or say **THANK YOU**.

That was **RUDE**. It was not the **POLITE** thing to do.

When it was time to show the paintings, Elephant didn't wait his turn. "Me first!" he shouted and **RUSHED** to Mrs Tree.

He didn't ask nicely and
he didn't say **PLEASE**.
That was **RUDE**. It was not
the **POLITE** thing to do.

Mrs Tree said patiently,
"Well done, Elephant."
She knew that was the
POLITE thing to do.

Next, Monkey showed everyone her painting. But Elephant didn't say, "Well done." Instead, he laughed, "That's silly! Monkey, you can't paint!"

That was a **RUDE** thing to say. It was not a **POLITE** thing to do.

But when Monkey started to **CRY**, Elephant realised he had not been **POLITE**. He had been very **RUDE**. Now he didn't know what to do.

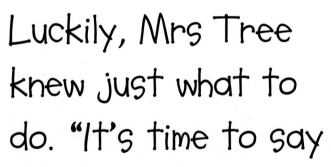

Luckily, Mrs Tree knew just what to do. "It's time to say sorry," she said. "You need to **THINK** before you speak."

Mrs Tree added, "It is easier to be **POLITE** than it is to be **RUDE.**"

Elephant **THOUGHT** about what he had done. Now he knew just what to do. "I'm sorry," Elephant whispered. It was a **POLITE** thing to do.

16

In the afternoon, during story time, Elephant sat and didn't make a sound. He listened very carefully, and even said **THANK YOU**.

At last, Elephant had learnt to be **POLITE!**

Words and feelings

Elephant was very rude in this story and that upset others.

POLITE

RUDE

PLEASE

In this book, there are a lot of words to do with being polite and rude, and how being rude can make others feel. Can you remember all of them?

CRY

UPSET

THANK YOU

Let's talk about behaviour

This series helps children to understand and manage difficult emotions and behaviours. The animal characters in the series have been created to show human behaviour that is often seen in young children, and which they may find difficult to manage.

Responding to Bad Manners

The story in this book examines issues around good manners. It looks at how people can be rude or polite, and how that makes others feel.

   The book is designed to show young children how they can manage their behaviour so they are polite to others.

How to use this book

You can read this book with one child or a group of children. The book can be used to begin a discussion around complex behaviour such as good manners.

   The book is also a reading aid, with enlarged and repeated words to help children to develop their reading skills.

How to read the story

Before beginning the story, ensure that the children you are reading to are relaxed and focused.

Take time to look at the enlarged words and the illustrations, and discuss what this book might be about before reading the story.

New words can be tricky for young children to approach. Sounding them out first, slowly and repeatedly, can help children to learn the words and become familiar with them.

How to discuss the story

When you have finished reading the story, use these questions and discussion points to examine the theme of the story with children and explore the emotions and behaviours within it:

- What do you think the story was about? Have you been rude or polite in a situation? What was that situation? For example, did you take a toy from another child without asking them if you could play with it first? Encourage the children to talk about their experiences.

- Talk about ways that people can learn to be polite and considerate. For example, try to always remember to say please and thank you when asking for things. Talk to the children about what tools they think might work for them and why.

- Discuss what it is like to cope with rudeness. Explain that Elephant was rude in the story and that upset the people around him. Elephant was rude because he did not consider others and their feelings.

- Talk about why it is important to say sorry to someone they have upset. Discuss why this can make that person feel better, and the person who says sorry feel better, too.

Titles in the series

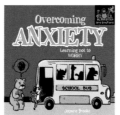

First published in 2023 by Fox Eye Publishing
Unit 31, Vulcan House Business Centre,
Vulcan Road, Leicester, LE5 3EF
www.foxeyepublishing.com

Copyright © 2023 Fox Eye Publishing
All rights reserved. No portion of this book may be
reproduced in any form without permission from the
publisher, except as permitted by U.K. copyright law.

Author: Jasmine Brooke
Art director: Paul Phillips
Cover designer: Emma Bailey & Salma Thadha
Editor: Jenny Rush

All illustrations by Novel

ISBN 978-1-80445-293-6

A catalogue record for this book is available from the
British Library

Printed in China